The
Underground
Hideaway

Murray Goodwin

Pictures by Peter Parnall

The
Underground
Hideaway

HARPER & ROW, PUBLISHERS
New York, Evanston, and London

To my son
FRANK

*The
Underground
Hideaway*

Chapter
1

Where in the world can they be taking me?
thought the little black-and-white animal as she
stuck her nose through the steel gate at the back
of the delivery truck.

She sniffed the night air. It held none of the
delicious fragrance of the country where she had
lived all her life. She poked her head out farther
through the metal gate and looked around. There
wasn't a tree to be seen! There were no fields, no
hills, no running brooks, no neat houses with
warm light spilling out the windows. The world
that met her anxious gaze was made of gray pavement and towering buildings. Menacing sounds
filled the air: the rumbles and roars of speeding

cars and trucks and the chilling blares of auto horns. It was a world she had never seen before.

The animal was a usually-cheerful skunk named Arletta. Only a few hours earlier things had begun to go wrong for her.

It had been just about time for an early dinner, and the little skunk was feeling a few small pangs of hunger. She was strolling across a well-tended lawn behind a trim white house with pink shutters. Arletta hoped to discover a tender chicken leg or a meaty ham bone in the garbage can near the back door. So intent was she on finding her dinner that she wasn't pre-pared for the attack of the beagle who sprang from the house, snarling and yelping.

The assault came as such a surprise that Arletta didn't have time to think of protecting herself with the odorous spray that skunks use as a defense. Instead, she scooted around a cop-per beech tree, wriggled through a picket fence, and scrambled onto the running board and through the open cab door of a department-store truck that had stopped to make a delivery. Hur-riedly she squeezed through the little square opening behind the driver's seat into the body of

the truck and wormed her way under a pile of mats in a corner.

Outside, the beagle danced around the truck, yapping in frustration. He was about to leap onto the front seat when the driver and his helper appeared.

"Scat! Scoot! Go home!" the driver yelled at him, clapping his hands loudly. The dog backed away, growling and whining. Arletta then heard the doors slam and the engine roar to life.

Now the truck began to jiggle as it picked up speed. Arletta fought her way out from under the mats and scurried to the back gate to peek out. To her dismay, she saw familiar things dwindle in the distance. The white house grew smaller and smaller. The picket fence had all but disappeared. Fields, hills, and trails she recognized swept by. All the places she loved dearly were falling far behind as the truck sped along. Feeling very forlorn, the skunk walked slowly back to the farthest corner and sat dejectedly on the mats. The ride seemed to go on forever.

At last Arletta felt the truck slow down, turn in a half circle, back up until it bumped lightly into something, and stop. The sound of the motor died, and the cab doors opened and then banged shut. Arletta heard one of the men walking toward the back of the truck. Quickly she struggled to hide herself under the mats again. The man opened the gate and flashed a light inside.

"Okay, Tom," he called to the other man, "it's empty." He turned off his flashlight and pulled the gate almost shut. From within her hiding place, Arletta heard the men walk away, their voices fading in the distance.

Arletta waited a long time before she crept out from under the mats. Carefully she made her way to the rear of the truck and peered out through the opening. A huge building, bigger than any house she had ever seen, stood before her. Where there should have been inviting green grass growing alongside the building, there stretched a dreary gray platform.

The first thing to do, thought Arletta, is to get out of here. Making herself as small as she could, the little skunk squeezed through the partly open gate and jumped down. Instinctively she scurried toward the building, but the solid wall held little protection. She followed the base of the building along the driveway to where the truck had turned in and finally arrived at the street. This side of the building had tall windows. Craning her neck to look through them, Arletta thought she could see humans standing stiffly and looking out of the windows, but not once did they move. Arletta crept along the base of the building until she came to a brass standpipe and stopped to consider her plight. In the dark she could not be seen so easily. But soon the night would become day, and in the daylight a lost skunk would be fair game for dogs, and even for some humans.

"Well," she said aloud, "what do I do *now*?" To her great surprise a voice answered her. Arletta leaped at the unexpected sound.

"Ah, little skunk. What you do now is come in here with the rest of us."

Arletta could hardly believe her ears. She looked left and right, but there was no one to be seen.

"Dear girl, look behind the pipe," the voice continued. "You'll see a large crack in the wall where the pipe enters the building. Crawl through the crack and follow the pipe down. It will lead you into a safe place; don't you worry."

Arletta made her decision very quickly. Anything would be better than wandering about out here, she thought. Into the crack she wriggled. Peering around, she could see the wide pipe that slanted downward for a few feet before it disappeared below a wall. Sitting on the pipe by the wall was a rather unusual animal. In the darkness Arletta could barely distinguish its features. It seemed to her that the animal was a cat, a very large cat indeed.

"Come, my dear," said the animal. "Crawl down the pipe, and follow me through this loose wallboard into our hideaway."

The animal waited while Arletta carefully made her way down the pipe.

"Now," said the animal, "watch me closely. When I push against the bottom of this wallboard, it will slide in and give me enough room to slip inside. I'll go first and show you how to do it. Please follow me in." The animal turned and leaned his weight against a wooden board in the wall. It moved inward, and he passed through the opening.

"See?" he said from within. "There's nothing to be afraid of. Just push on the board."

Arletta put her front paws on the loose board. It gave way more easily than she had expected. Arletta slipped through nervously, not knowing what to expect on the other side. She found herself in a large room. Opposite the wall with the loose board was a door that stood open a few inches. Around the door and through a glass transom above it, a dim light was shining into the room.

The little skunk took a few hesitant steps and peered around. The room was filled with all sorts of things, many of which she recognized from her country prowls to barns and garages and sheds. The tools hanging neatly on one wall were a familiar sight. So was the table along another wall. And the small barrels and paint buckets under it. Cartons and boxes were scattered helter-skelter on the floor and piled high along the walls.

Standing in the middle of the room, watching her, was the animal who had led her indoors. He was a cat, the largest, fattest cat Arletta had ever seen. She stared at him. His body, covered with beautiful long gray hair, was so enormous it almost reached the ground. His head was huge and perfectly round. From it rose long and neatly tapered ears. His eyes, large in the dim light, were a startling, bright orange.

"Welcome," said the cat. "Welcome to our hideaway in the depths of The Mart."

Before Arletta had a chance to reply, a rat slunk out from behind a box and crouched alongside the big cat. He did not seem at all afraid.

Looking at the skunk with dark beady eyes, he said sourly, "Oh, here's another one."

The cat glanced at the rat beside him, then turned his attention back to Arletta.

"Allow me to introduce ourselves. My name is Staten Island Fats. My ratty companion is a Norway rat named Erik. If you are wondering why I—a cat—do not devour him—a rat—there are several reasons."

"Oh, come on, Fats!" snapped the rat. "Just give her the facts, and let's get it over with."

The cat ignored the interruption. "First of all, I work during the day in a fine butcher shop down the street, where I have my fill of prime tidbits, so a scrawny rat doesn't tempt me for a minute. Secondly, this room is an animal hideaway, and any animal who enters this hideaway is a friend to any other animal here."

"Friends," muttered the rat. "Who's got friends in this world?" He looked sharply at Arletta. "Do you have a name? Or do we just call you skunk? And do you have any questions?"

Arletta studied the rat closely. He was a muddy brown-gray color, like dirty water. His

head was long and thin, with closely-set little cropped ears. His black eyes were never still, darting suspiciously from side to side. He had straggly grayish whiskers that moved up and down when he wiggled his nose, which was quite often. His skinny, hairless tail, wrapped around him, was easily as long as his body.

"A name? Of course I have a name. It's Arletta. And of course I have questions. The first one is what's a mart? And what's a hideaway?"

"*The* Mart, not *a* mart," said the rat disgustedly. "The Mart is the name of the department store in whose subbasement storeroom you're standing, skunk. It happens to be in the Bronx, northernmost borough of New York City."

"New York City?" cried Arletta unbelievingly. "You mean to tell me I'm in New York City?"

"What's wrong with New York City?" snarled the rat. "Just so happens I was born in New York City."

"Erik, Erik," reproached Staten Island Fats, "must you display your ratty nature all the time? Can't you see you are upsetting our new guest? She's lost and she's frightened."

The enormous cat turned back to the young

skunk. "Be calm, my dear. You are in good hands. My guess would be that you came from the suburbs north of here—probably Westchester County. We have had some fine guests from that part of the country staying in our hideaway from time to time. I myself came from Staten Island. And under rather trying circumstances."

"Everything about that fat cat is big," mumbled the rat, "even the words he uses."

Staten Island Fats ignored him. "I was born in a big house on Staten Island that a city family had rented for the summer. Their children enjoyed me as a kitten, and I was going to be the family pet. I had a fine time with the youngsters all summer, but when it was over and the family was driving back to their city apartment, they decided I was getting too big to live with them any more. So they just tossed me out of the car not far from here." The cat's orange eyes narrowed at the memory of the cruelty.

"Well," said the rat, "that's the human race for you."

Arletta asked, "How do you happen to be here?"

"I had a most fortunate stroke of luck," replied Staten Island Fats. "Later that day the little daughter of the man who owns the butcher shop picked me up and took me home to live with them. But while I was out on that street, alone and with nowhere to go, I was terribly frightened, so I know what it means to be without a home and friends. That's why I decided to be a friend to every lost animal I met. And that's how I happened to start this hideaway."

"So you and Erik share this room together?" asked Arletta.

"Oh, there are a few more of us," said the rat, looking disgusted. "You haven't met Norton, the Virginia opossum. He's a real fancy gentleman, our Norton. Always bowing to the ladies, paying compliments. Sometimes he's so polite he makes me sick."

"These days," interjected the cat, "Norton pays his compliments to Ginger, the only lady staying with us right now. She's a flying squirrel. You two will like each other, I'm sure."

"Do you all live here? In this storeroom underneath a department store?" Arletta could barely hide her surprise.

"Well," explained Staten Island Fats, "it's more of a stopping-off place than a home. It's a refuge. A—a *hideaway*—a place where lost animals can safely stay until they decide where they are going to settle permanently. It's peaceful here, and food is plentiful as you will discover."

The fat cat took long, graceful strides until he stood quite near Arletta. "Excuse me, please," he apologized. "This is no time to chatter away. You must be weary and hungry. Let us find you a comfortable burrow, and then Erik will show you the way to our dining room."

Staten Island Fats stalked around the room, carefully studying the boxes on the floor. Arletta followed him, sniffing at everything she passed. The big cat stopped in front of a square pink box with large gay flowers on it.

"Ah," he said, "here's a pretty one. And just the right size for you."

Erik snorted. "Comes from the Ladies' Hats department. Wait till you see those funny-looking hats." He shuddered.

Arletta paid no attention to him. "I'd love to claim it if no one else is using it," she said to Staten Island Fats.

"It's all yours, Arletta," said the cat.

"Last one to use it was a dumb bunny," cackled Erik. "Dumb! He was so dumb he let himself get trapped in the revolving door upstairs."

"That's enough of that sort of talk, Erik,"

14

said the cat sternly. "I think it would be a good idea if you gave Arletta a tour of The Mart, and then escorted her to our dining room."

"All right, all right. Come on, skunk. I could use a snack myself."

Rudely, the rat scurried out through the door ahead of Arletta. In the hallway he said, "We walk up this ramp to the basement. After we look around there, I'll take you up to the main floor on the *funny* stairs."

"What's funny about them?" asked Arletta.

"They move. All by themselves. Lazy humans use them to get carried up to the next floor. Humans!" he said scornfully. "Too lazy to walk up a flight of steps."

Erik scuttled up the ramp leading to the basement with Arletta right behind him. "Always walk close to the wall," he advised her. "Makes it harder for the humans to see you. I doubt that any of them will be around here at this hour of the night—although you never can tell about humans. Can't trust them for a minute!"

Chapter
2

They came out into the basement, and Arletta gasped at what she saw. The rat's face held only a look of contempt.

"Junk!" he snapped. "Stuff and junk. The junky stuff humans clutter up their lives with. But if you want to look at it, stick with me and I'll show you around."

With Arletta close behind, Erik scuttled along the aisles, pointing out shiny pots and pans hanging on walls, silky curtains on racks, drab work clothes piled high on counters, glittering imitation jewelry in glass cases, and waxy artificial flowers in plastic vases. From time to time, the little skunk stood on her hind legs and craned her head so that she could see everything. Her eyes danced at the unaccustomed sights.

Erik's lips were twisted in a sneer. *"Pah!"* he exploded. "Enough of this junk! Come on. We'll go up the funny stairs to the main floor." He led Arletta to the escalator steps.

"They're not moving," Arletta observed.

"They only move during the day," Erik explained, "when the lazy humans are here."

They climbed the high steps one by one. Erik had to leap up each step; Arletta hoisted herself slowly on her short legs. "I hope it's easier coming down," she panted. At last they came to the top step. Arletta paused to catch her breath.

"Let's go! Let's go!" urged the rat. "I haven't got all night!"

Arletta trotted along behind him as he went up one aisle and down the next, describing the different articles as they came to them. Erik showed her ladies' dresses and coats, men's suits, ties, gloves, scarves, and hats. Arletta stopped to sniff at the perfume counter. Erik's thin long nose quivered with distaste. "Who needs it? Come on, skunk. Up we go."

They climbed another flight of escalator steps to the second floor. Erik paraded Arletta around the counters, showing her electric dishwashers, electric knives, electric can-openers, electric hair-dryers, electric toothbrushes, and electric typewriters. "These are for lazy people just like the ones who can't walk upstairs. Let's go up to the *good* floor—where the food is."

When they reached the top step the rat said, "I'll take you around before we go to the dining room." He scooted along an aisle. "Here's the game department. Toys and dolls. Baseballs and footballs. Tennis balls and golf balls. And look at this! Stuffed animals humans buy for their kids to play with." He shuddered. "Ugh! Gives me the creeps! Let's get away from here."

They moved along. "This is the pet shop. Here's where humans buy diamond-studded collars for poodles and fur coats for Pekingese. Also cages for canaries." He snorted. Erik led Arletta past a fish aquarium. "Good place for a drink," he pointed out, "but let's get on to the food."

He showed the little skunk the way to the food department. "Here we are," said the rat with a touch of pride, pointing to the delicacies. "Meats of all kinds—for all tastes. In these glass cases, you see salami, liverwurst, bacon, and many varieties of ham, roast beef, frankfurters, baloney, and sausages. On those counters"—he waved grandly—"cheeses from all over. Nuts, fish, fruit—you name it, we have it." He grinned broadly at Arletta. She was enthralled by it all.

"And now, follow me. I will take you to our private dining room. It's a little storage room where they put broken food jars, crumbled pieces of cheese, smashed-open boxes of fruit, and chunks of meat they have cut by mistake. Humans make lots of mistakes, so you can be sure what we find is fresh every day," he said with a smirk.

He led the way behind a counter to a swinging door that opened into the storage room. He leaned against the door, and as it swung open he slipped inside. "Push," he called from within. "It opens easily."

Arletta put her paws against the door and scrunched through. Erik was already sitting on the floor in the corner beside a large barrel filled with delicacies from broken boxes and smashed jars.

"Help yourself," said the rat, "but don't take all night. If you think I'm going to play nursemaid to a skunk, you're crazy!" He scuttled up into the barrel, and Arletta could hear him rummaging around inside. Soon he emerged with a large slice of Swiss-cheese rind in his mouth. He scrabbled to a corner of the room and nibbled away.

Arletta remembered that she hadn't had any dinner. She found a broken can of Danish bacon and took a few slices, then settled down near Erik to enjoy them. In between dainty bites, she asked, "Does Mr. Fats come up here with you?"

"Fats? Nah. Never. Why should he? He gets all he can eat in that fancy butcher shop of his. Once in awhile I take him some catnip from the pet shop. It's a treat."

"And the others?"

"Well, that Norton sure loves to eat. But he's such a coward he doesn't like to come up here by himself. He'd rather fish around in garbage cans outdoors, late at night, when no humans are around."

"And Ginger?"

"Oh, she takes care of herself, all right. But never mind the chatter. Finish your dinner and let's get going."

Arletta brushed her mouth daintily with a paw and said, "Ready whenever you are, Erik."

"Well," snapped the rat, "what are we waiting for? Now, on the way down, let's see if you can make it on your own, right back into the hideaway. I'm not going to spend my life giving guided tours around here.''

"All right, follow me!" Arletta said cheerfully, as she trotted off through the aisles to the top of the stairs. Without hesitation she went down floor after floor, with the rat racing along behind her. Hurrying into the subbasement, she sped along the corridor and into the hideaway. There was no one in sight. Then Staten Island Fats spoke up from behind the door.

"Ah, my dear, welcome back. You're just in time to meet Ginger." He stepped out to the middle of the room and looked up toward the top of the highest stack of cartons. "Come show yourself, Ginger!" he called. "Fly down and meet our new guest. Arletta just arrived tonight from the country."

As Arletta followed his glance she saw a tiny brown animal, no bigger than a chipmunk, appear at the edge of the carton. She peered curiously at Arletta.

"Excuse me for asking," inquired Arletta politely, "but can you *really* fly—like a bird?"

"Like a bird, no. Like a flying squirrel, yes," answered Ginger. "Actually, I *glide*. We flying squirrels can only fly downward." The little squirrel looked at Arletta with large brown eyes.

"I don't mean to brag," she said modestly, "but I can sail quite far."

"My!" exclaimed the skunk. "Could you show me? I mean—not to be rude—next time you take off on a flight, could you let me know?"

"No trouble at all. Happy to do it right now," said Ginger. "Watch!"

The tiny squirrel huddled into a tight ball, her feet close together. With a sudden spring she leaped from the carton, spread her four legs wide, and soared downward toward Arletta. Near the ground she flipped her tail upward to reduce her speed and landed with a graceful plop right next to the skunk.

"How wonderful!" cried Arletta with admiration. "I've never seen anything like that before!"

"Wonderful my tail," muttered Erik. "How come nobody ever says 'wonderful!' when a rat does something nice?"

Ginger turned to the rat. "Something nice indeed," she said tartly. "Name one nice thing you've done. Name *one*!"

Staten Island Fats broke in. "Ladies, gentlemen, remember where we are. This squabbling is quite unbecoming."

Suddenly the big cat stiffened. His head

came up alertly and his ears twitched. The other animals held their breath and watched him. "I hear something," he said softly. "Quick! To your hiding places! And quiet, all of you!"

Within a moment the rat had scuttled to the far corner of the room behind a leg of the table, and Ginger had climbed back up the stack of cartons. Arletta plunged into the box that was now her new burrow and huddled there, listening. Only the huge cat stayed out in the open. Carefully, his body hugging the ground as if he were stalking prey, he made his way to the slightly open door. He crouched behind it, with his ears flattened against his head and his claws extended, ready to pounce.

The sounds outside the room could be clearly heard by all the animals now. Something was making its way down the incline in a hurry. Noisy running steps echoed along the corridor and grew louder just outside the door.

Shivering in her box, Arletta heard the intruder hurtle into the room with a clatter and a thump. There was a deadly silence. Then she heard Staten Island Fats speak. "Oh, it's you," he said witheringly. "I should have guessed."

"Come on out, everybody," called Staten Island Fats, his voice heavy with annoyance. "It's our roommate, making his usual dramatic entrance."

Arletta poked her head cautiously out of her box. She saw a frizzy gray-white heap lying on the floor, panting heavily. About half the size of Staten Island Fats, he had a long-snouted face that now wore a woebegone expression. His eyes were closed and his tongue lolled out of his mouth. Except for his heavy breathing, he might have been taken for dead.

Arletta looked up at Staten Island Fats inquiringly. "Norton?" she asked.

"Norton," replied the big cat dryly.

At the sound of her voice, the opossum opened his eyes slowly, lifted his head, and looked in Arletta's direction. He beamed at the sight of her and leaped to his feet.

"Well, I do declare, ma'am," he drawled. "Another beautiful lady joins our group."

"There he goes again," said Erik rudely as he slunk out from behind the table leg. "Mr. Charming."

The opossum paid no attention to him. "May I be allowed to introduce myself, ma'am? The name is Norton, of the Virginia opossums, I am proud to say."

"My name is Arletta," said the skunk softly, melting under Norton's charm.

"Arletta," said the opossum, looking thoughtful. "Arletta. The name has a southern ring to it. Are you from the great Southland?"

Ginger soared down from her perch on the pile of cartons. "No, Norton, she's from the great Northland. Northern Westchester, if you must know."

The opossum fixed a warm glance on the skunk. "Ah, ma'am, no matter. We're delighted to have you here. A charming addition to our little group. You'll find us rather appealing in our differences, I'm sure. I, for one, am gallant,

25

amusing, polite, and somewhat of a coward."

"You can say that again," muttered Erik. "For an animal that has more than fifty teeth, he sure is afraid of his own shadow."

"I prefer to use all those teeth for eating," replied Norton loftily. He turned back to Arletta. "I'm hungry *all* the time, you see. Just now, while I was getting a breath of fresh air, I couldn't resist looking into one of the garbage cans. I *love* to look into garbage cans. Unfortunately, this one was empty. Through some mischance, I happened to fall into it, and I couldn't get out! It took me ages to tip the can over. Then I ran back here as fast as I could. Imagine my delight at finding you here!"

Staten Island Fats looked severely at him. "Do you know how many house rules you've broken, Norton?"

The opossum looked contrite. "Please accept my apologies, sir. It is my unfortunate nature to be hungry and cowardly at the same time."

The flying squirrel turned to the enormous cat. "Hadn't you better get back to the butcher shop? It will be opening soon."

"Yes, thank you, my dear. In my absence, will you explain the house rules to Arletta?" The cat walked to the loose wallboard. "I hope to see you all this evening if I can possibly get away. Please be careful.'' The cat then wedged his huge body through the loose wallboard.

The rat watched with amusement. "One of these days that fat cat will get so fat that he's going to get stuck in the wall."

Soon after the departure of Staten Island Fats, Ginger scrambled to the top of the table and called: "All right, everybody, gather round. I'm going to explain the house rules to Arletta, and it won't hurt the rest of you to listen."

"Rules, rules," snorted the rat. "Who has to live by the rules?"

"Why, Erik, we all do," said Ginger. "That's how we protect one another." She turned to Arletta. "You may not know it, but an awful lot of animals find their way to New York City. Some get here by accident, the way you did; others wander away from their homes."

"Some even escape from zoos," added Norton. "I happen to know."

"Right around New York," continued Ginger, "you'll find woodchucks, raccoons, rabbits, and mink. Once in awhile, you'll see a beaver. And I heard of a black bear who has been seen roaming the streets of a town just across the

Hudson River. So I guess we're lucky to have a hideaway like this to save us from the dangers outside.''

"I'll say there's danger outside," groused Erik. "Do you know how many nasty stray cats there are in New York? Seventy thousand, that's how many. And every one of them is looking for me.''

"Well," said Ginger philosophically, "we all have our troubles.'' She gazed down at the skunk. "We don't have many rules, Arletta, but the ones we have are *all* important. The first is that we never turn away or attack any creature that comes to our hideaway looking for shelter.''

"Well, I'm grateful for *that* rule," said Arletta.

"Next," continued Ginger, "once you are in here, you must never do anything to put the others in danger. For example, if you happen to be seen outside this room by a human, don't lead him back here where the rest of us are hiding.''

"A very sensible rule," observed Arletta.

"Third, we eat only during the night or very early in the morning—when there are no humans around. And we *never* eat in the hideaway.''

"Of course," agreed Arletta. "I understand."

"And finally, never leave the hideaway without telling one of the others where you are going."

"Don't worry. I'll never break *that* rule," said the skunk with a small shiver.

Ginger looked at her with warm and friendly eyes. "Do you have any questions, Arletta?"

"Just one, Ginger," she said with a sigh. "Do you think I'll ever get back to the country again?"

"To the country!" exclaimed Norton. "Why would you ever want to go back? I know I wouldn't. Not after the terrible time I had!"

"Here it comes," snapped Erik. "Now we have to hear the story of his hard life."

Norton shuffled closer to Arletta. "Well, it's true. Do you know the kind of childhood an opossum has? Miserable! When I was born, fifteen brothers and sisters were born with me. Fifteen! We were so small you could fit us all on a rose petal. At first we lived in our mother's pouch."

"Her *pouch*?" inquired Arletta.

"Yes, ma'am. A little pocket in front of her.

And let me tell you, jiggling around in a pouch with fifteen brothers and sisters is no joy ride.''

The opossum got to his feet and strode up and down dramatically. ''What a desperate struggle it was for my poor mother to feed us all! When we got a little older, we climbed out of her pouch and onto her back. We hung on, trying to help her look for food. We never had enough to eat. Never!''

''What happened?'' asked Arletta.

''What happened, ma'am? Why, one by one we fell off my mother's back, and from then on we were on our own in the cruel world, tiny as we were!''

There was a polite silence after Norton finished his story. Then Arletta remarked, ''I'm sorry to hear of your troubles, Norton, but *I* would like to get back to the outdoors. I really would.''

''Well, ma'am, if that's your heart's desire,'' said the opossum, ''I'll see that you get it.'' Erik the rat snorted.

Ginger jumped down from the table and scurried to the door where she cocked her head to listen. ''Hush!'' she called out. ''I think the humans have just opened the store.''

She came back to Arletta. ''Time for us all

to settle down now. Don't be alarmed if you hear noises from above."

"Do the humans ever come down here?" asked Arletta in a frightened voice.

"Oh, once in awhile. But we always hear them coming, and we scoot through the wall before they get here."

The squirrel walked with Arletta to her hat-box burrow. "The first day away from home is always the hardest," she said sympathetically, "but soon you won't mind it at all. Get some sleep now. You look like you need it."

Chapter
4

Erik the rat was restless. He grunted, gnashed his teeth, swore to himself, and thought about how he hated everybody. Finally, with an explosive *"Pah!"* he gave up the whole idea of sleep and called to Norton.

"Norton. Hey, Norton, you asleep?"

The opossum, dreaming that he was about to bite into a juicy apple, slowly opened his eyes. "Not any more, I would like to tell you. What can I do for you, sir?"

"I think I'll go out for a swim. The rules say I got to tell someone. So I'm telling you I'm going out for a swim."

"A swim!" exclaimed the opossum with disgust. "You call splashing around in a filthy sewer going for a swim?"

"Well, that's where I'm going." The rat crouched in his corner and debated which route to take to his favorite sewer. If he went through the wallboard, he would come out on the street at the standpipe. That would give him a fine chance to terrify any humans who happened to be passing by. On the other hand, if he stayed indoors and went up the incline to the subbasement, he could slip through a hole which led from the air-conditioning duct right out to the corner where the sewer was. He decided to stay indoors.

Cautiously he poked his head out the door and looked both ways. Even though the store hadn't opened yet, there might be some store humans around. No one was in sight. He slunk up the dimly-lit incline leading to the basement. Hugging the wall, he was about halfway up when two young men in denim pants and sweat shirts started down, each pushing a handtruck. They were on their way to the hideaway for some supplies.

Humans! the rat thought to himself. Listen to them! Joking and whistling as though they didn't have a care in the world. Making enough noise to rattle the teeth of the animals in the hideaway. I'll fix them, Erik thought with satisfaction.

He scuttled noisily along the incline directly toward the young workmen and squeaked loudly. *"Creek! Creek!"* he whined, pretending to be frightened. *"Creek!"*

The workmen failed to hear him. What's the matter with them? thought the rat. Are they deaf as well as dumb? In a bold move he skittered close to one of the young men, squeaking *"Creek! Creek! Creek!"* as loudly as he could. And still they kept coming and talking to each other, unaware of the presence of the rat. Erik was infuriated. If there was one thing he hated, it was to be ignored by a human. In a frenzy, the rat hurled himself against the leg of one of the young men, then backed away. The man looked down, and his mouth opened in surprise. "Jeepers, Charlie, looka here! A rat! A rat! Let's get him!"

They let go of their handtrucks, which began to roll down the incline with a deafening clatter. One of the young men pulled a hammer from the back pocket of his pants and began to chase Erik. Up and down the incline the rat raced, back and forth from wall to wall, in and out between the men's legs, laughing inwardly as they kicked at

him or swung the hammer wildly. Beginning to tire of the game, Erik scuttled up the incline, turned sharply to the right, and popped into a little hole in the wall behind a pair of rubber boots in the men's footwear department. The workmen came after him but slowed down as they neared the basement level. The store had just opened, and they did not want to alarm any of the customers. With furtive glances, they searched along the aisles and the counters. One of them shifted the pair of rubber boots which Erik had slipped past on his way to the hole. Observing the scene from just inside the hole, Erik hugged his sides with joy. What a wonderful way to start the morning! Filled with happiness, he watched the two humans give up the search, then continued on his way for a leisurely swim in the sewer.

Chapter
5

The moment they heard the terrible crashing sounds of the handtrucks clattering down the incline, the animals fled from the hideaway through the loose wallboard. They crouched on the pipe, tense and listening. Just when they thought the crisis had passed, they heard voices from within the hideaway.

Ginger sat on her haunches, her front paws held closely together. Arletta sat right behind Ginger, her tail curved and her head cocked to one side, listening intently to the men's voices as if she could understand them. Beyond her sat Norton, pretending to be calm for the ladies' sake, but inside wishing to run off somewhere and play dead.

Inside the hideaway, the two men were busy setting rattraps in different parts of the room.

"Here's a good place, Bud," said the young man named Charlie. "Right between these two barrels under the table. When that rat smells this cheese and sticks his nose in here—*Kazoom!* One dead rat!"

"Yeah," said Bud. "And if he misses that one, wait till he snoops around the leg of the table in this corner. *Plowee!* The living end!"

Behind the wall, the animals sat in horrified silence. Although they could not understand a single word, they knew by the tone of the voices that something very unpleasant was being planned for them. Arletta listened with apprehension to the cunning voices, the harsh laughter and, at long last, the sounds of footsteps leaving the room and growing fainter as the men went upstairs.

"They've gone," said Ginger.

"Wait, wait," said Arletta. "Let's stay out here for awhile longer until we are absolutely sure they've gone."

"Nonsense," the little squirrel said, "they've gone. But if it will make you feel any better, Norton will peek in and scout around, won't you, Norton?"

A woebegone expression crossed the opossum's face. "Of course, ma'am, I'd be delighted, simply *charmed* to have a look, *if* you think it is necessary at this *particular* time. However, there is a good deal of merit," he added cheerfully, "to Arletta's suggestion that we give them a mite more time. Just a mite. Mightn't we?" he asked hopefully.

"Humph!" said the little flying squirrel. "Sit here and keep Arletta company. I'll sneak back in and look things over from the top of my stack. If everything seems all right, I'll let you know."

"Ma'am," said the Virginia opossum admiringly, "you have the brains to match your beauty—both of them real."

"And you have the courage to match your charm," replied Ginger, "both false." With a flip of her tail, the squirrel turned and scurried down the pipe.

They watched her disappear through the opening and heard her scramble up her stack of boxes. For a few moments there was silence. Then they heard a whooshing sound as Ginger glided from the top of the stack to the floor and ran from one corner of the room to the other. Again there was silence. At last, the squirrel called: "All right. You can come back, but be careful."

Norton turned to Arletta with a gallant bow. "After you, ma'am," he said.

Arletta pushed through the loose board and looked around. "Come in," said Ginger. "Just stay in the middle of the room until I point something out to you."

The skunk came into the room with Norton on her heels. They stood quietly.

"Over there in Erik's corner is something that wasn't there before. It has cheese in it. And between the barrels where you like to stay, Norton, is another horrible contraption—also with cheese."

"Food!" exclaimed Norton, moving toward the trap between the barrels. "Well, bless their human hearts! Cheese! Just in time for a snack."

"Norton!" screamed Ginger, and the opossum jumped in alarm. "Be careful! They *want* you to eat the cheese, and then something *dreadful* would probably happen to you."

The opossum hastily retreated from the trap. "Well, I do declare!" said Norton with a shudder. "All of a sudden I've lost my appetite!"

"I'm also afraid the men will be back soon to see the results of their work," said Ginger, looking rather grim. "I don't like any of this. I wish Staten Island Fats were here."

"Don't you worry," said the opossum. "*I'm* not going near that—whatever it is. And I don't believe they'll be back soon. They'll want to give us time to get careless."

"Or greedy," said Ginger, and looked at Norton.

"Well, that will give us time to talk this over with Mr. Fats, won't it?" asked Arletta. "He'll know what's best for us."

"In the meantime, ladies," said Norton, "let's get some rest. All this excitement's tuckered me out. I think I'll find me another resting place." He looked around the room and finally chose a cozy den in the angle formed by two boxes that were close to each other. "I'm a little tired, I must say. And a mite hungry."

Arletta said, "Well, Norton, keep your mind off that cheese. Just shut your eyes and pick out something nice to think about."

"Yes ma'am," agreed the opossum, closing

his eyes. "I'm now thinking about something nice."

"Good," said Arletta. "What is it?"

"Cheese," answered the opossum dreamily.

One by one, the animals dozed off. Ginger was out of sight, perched in the far corner of the tallest stack of cartons. Arletta retired to her box, dreaming about the country. In her dream the beagle who had started her on this adventure had just apologized and was now offering to share a turkey gizzard that he had found in a loose-lidded garbage can.

The exhausted animals slept most of the afternoon, until their peace was disturbed by a clattering sound. In the center of the room stood Erik, a crazy grin on his face.

"Well, where is everybody?"

"Hush up, Erik!" snapped Ginger. "Don't move until I come down. I've got something to show you."

As Ginger soared down Arletta and Norton gathered around the rat. "Wait till I tell you what happened to me!" Erik kept repeating. "Boy! Did I have fun with a couple of humans before I had my swim."

"Oh! So that's it!" said Ginger. "That's why they came in here and left those funny things with the cheese." She tossed her head at the one in Erik's corner. "Look!"

The rat swaggered toward his favorite corner for a closer look. "Oh, that!" he said with indifference. "It's a rattrap. I know all about those. When I lived in an apartment house, I saw them all the time." He stepped a little closer to the trap and sniffed. "Cheese! Ah, they brought me some cheese. Isn't that nice!"

"Don't touch it, Erik!" cried Arletta. "It was put there by two humans who were laughing over it."

"Them!" said the rat scornfully. "I ran into those two earlier. And did they give *me* something to laugh over!" With chortles and snorts, the rat described his adventure with the workmen. When he had finished, Arletta recounted the fearful events that had taken place in the room earlier in the day. As they talked, the noises in the store above began to die down. There were fewer footsteps and less talking.

Ginger cocked her tiny head to one side. "Must be near closing time. Soon we'll have the place to ourselves."

Erik kept slinking back and forth in front of the trap in his corner. Every once in awhile he snorted. Occasionally a ratty chuckle would come out of his mouth. Suddenly he stopped and turned to Norton. "Nort, you old Southern gent, how would you like to help me play a joke on those trap-setters?" He wriggled his tail evilly. "How about it, Nort?"

The opossum eyed him suspiciously. "Well, sir," he said, "I'm all in favor of a touch of humor. I enjoy the sound of laughter. I'll go along with you. *But* not if it can be dangerous for the ladies."

"Dangerous?" snorted the rat. "Not a chance. Now come over here by this trap, and I'll show you what I have in mind."

Chapter 6

With fear in his heart, the opossum walked over to Erik, who sat beside the trap in his favorite corner. Ginger and Arletta were too inquisitive not to gather around as well. The rat surveyed them with a cocky eye.

"In a minute, friends," he said with a smirk, "all of us are going to nibble on some cheese. Norton and I will get it for you."

Arletta gasped. "You mean you are going to snatch the cheese? Are you crazy?"

"Crazy like a Norway rat," cackled Erik. "Climb into that barrel, Nort, and get me one of those long iron nails." Erik seemed to enjoy being in charge for once.

"A pleasure, sir," said the opossum, scrambling into the barrel. A few seconds later he peered over the rim, with a long nail in his hand-like paw. "Will this do, sir?"

"That's perfect, Nort, perfect!" the rat said heartily. "Now come back down here, and I'll show you what to do."

The opossum stared unhappily at the rat. "Must I?" he said.

"Ah, come on now, Nort. Are you an opossum or a mouse? There's nothing to be afraid of." He pointed his nose at the cheese. "What the humans want us to do is to nibble at the cheese. But what *they* don't know," he sneered, "is that *I* know that the cheese is attached to that big spring on the back of the trap and that pulling at the cheese unhooks the spring. And before you can say 'yum, yum,' it comes down *wham* on your neck."

The opossum winced. "Erik, you promised me I wouldn't be doing anything dangerous!"

The rat pointed at the long nail Norton was holding. "It won't be. Not with that. All you do is stand right here, poke at the cheese with the nail, and then quickly pull it back. The spring comes down on nothing." He paused dramatically. "Then I walk over, take out the cheese, and we have a little feast. A feast for us and a big puzzle for the trap-setters." He looked around at Arletta and Ginger. "A cinch. And a great joke."

"They'll hear the noise," said Ginger.

"Who will?" asked the rat. "The store's closed. Everybody is gone."

"Isn't it easier just to go upstairs and get some food?" asked Arletta. "Anyway, if we don't touch the cheese, if we just stay away from the traps for a few days, they'll think there is no one down here. Wouldn't that be better?"

The rat glared at her. "Listen to that skunk!" he snarled. "Her first day here and she's telling everybody what's what!"

The flying squirrel snapped, "She happens to be right, that's what!"

Disgustedly, the rat turned toward Norton. "What about it, Norton? Do you want to have some fun? Or are you going to go along with the girlies?"

The opossum blinked, shuffled his feet, wiggled his hairless tail, and stared at the steel spring of the rattrap.

"Fun is fun, Erik. I'm all for that, indeed I am. But let's not lose our heads over a joke."

He recoiled in horror at the thought of what he had just said. "I mean, let's let sleeping dogs lie."

The rat seared him with a look. "You're a disgrace to the animal world, Norton. You know what I think?" he jeered. "I think you're a coward."

"There's a big difference between being a coward and a fool," observed Ginger.

"Don't let yourself get talked into something you'll regret," advised Arletta.

The opossum shook his head uncertainly. How he wished he could be a hero with the ladies! If only he weren't so frightened! He looked at the cheese in the trap. It looked delicious. He looked at the spring on the trap. It looked deadly. He looked at Norton. The rat glared back with loathing.

The opossum made up his mind. "All right, Erik. We'll do it."

"Now you're talking," approved the rat. "Get in a little closer with the nail and poke it at the cheese."

Norton wiggled the nail and approached the trap. Ginger and Arletta watched in horror.

"Better stand back a little, ladies," said the

opossum. "I wouldn't want anything to happen to you pretty creatures."

The two little animals backed away slowly to the loose wallboard. They couldn't take their eyes from the nail held in the opossum's paw. Norton approached the trap cautiously, holding the nail as far out as he could. Erik stood by not far from the trap.

"Just touch it, Nort," he advised, "and pull it back fast."

The opossum got as close to the trap as he dared. He stared at the steel spring and shuddered. Then, gathering his courage, he suddenly reached out with the nail, tapped the cheese with it, and pulled the nail back quickly.

The released spring snapped down. *Crack!* At the terrible sound, Norton leaped into the air, then crumpled to the floor as if he were dead. Arletta leaped into her box and lay quivering. Ginger squeaked and fled out through the loose board. Erik sat back on his haunches and laughed.

"All right, all right, it's all over. Come on out and watch this," said Erik. He swaggered up to the trap, put his front paws on the now harmless spring, looked back at the animals, and then,

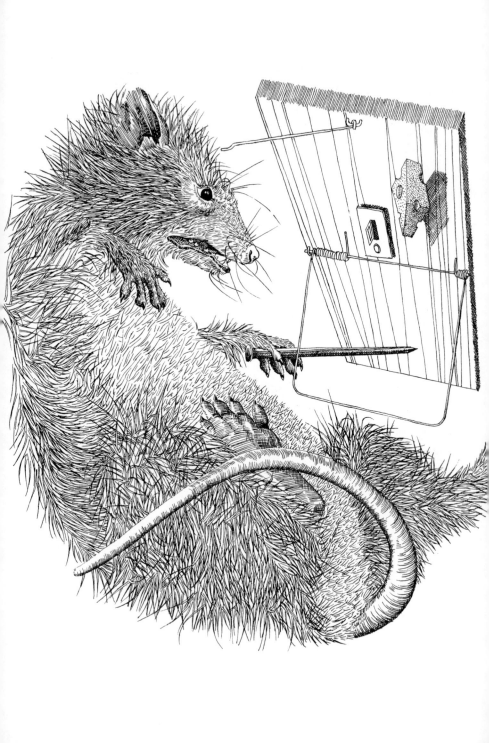

very casually, he reached in and took the cheese out of the trap with his teeth. His beady eyes were filled with ratty pleasure. Triumphantly he placed the cheese in the middle of the floor.

"All right, Norton. Let's get the second one." He pointed at the trap between Norton's favorite barrels.

The opossum, who hadn't stopped shaking since the first trap went off, sat in a lump beside the table leg. "Well, sir," he said, "if you'll kindly allow me to catch my breath."

The rat flashed him a look of annoyance. "Want a piece of cheese?" he asked nastily. "You'll have to work for it."

With a long drawn-out sigh, the opossum picked up the nail he had dropped in his fright and walked reluctantly toward the trap between the barrels. Again he jabbed out. Again the spring cracked down with a nerve-shaking snap.

Cockily, the rat strutted to the trap and withdrew the bait. "Norton, you share your piece with Ginger. I'll divide mine with our visitor from the country."

"Thanks just the same," said Arletta weakly. "But I seem to have lost my appetite."

"So have I," said Ginger.

"Suit yourself," said the rat.

"Please, ladies," implored Norton. "Do join us." Now that the crisis was over, his spirits were bubbling. In fact, he felt rather heroic about the whole incident. He looked at Erik and shrugged elaborately. "Well, if they won't, they won't."

The opossum lay down in his favorite spot with his legs lying across the sprung trap. "My congratulations to you, sir, for thinking up this extraordinary plan. And just in time for snacks."

Erik sprawled in his corner, munching his morsel. "Nothing to it," he said, chewing noisily. He smacked his lips and looked slyly at Arletta and Ginger.

"Boy! This is *some* cheese. I've had all kinds of cheese in my day—hard cheese, soft cheese, smelly cheese, blue cheese, red cheese—but I don't remember any of them tasting as good as this rat-trap cheese." He spun around and looked right at Norton. "And do you know why?"

The opossum shuffled around uncomfortably. "Well, sir, I can't rightfully say that I do," he answered.

"I'll tell you why. Because by taking this

cheese from the trap-setters we have struck a small blow at the human race."

Arletta said, "What's so bad about humans? Where I come from, I see them take very good care of their cats and dogs and other pets. They brush their horses; they feed the birds in the winter. In fact, animals are pretty lucky to be living in the country."

"Bah!" exploded the rat. "The country! The country! Can't you ever talk about anything but the country?" He jerked his head at the opossum. "C'mon, buddy, I'm thirsty. Let's wash down this rat-trap cheese with some good cold city water. Then we'll take a stroll around the store."

Norton leaped to his feet. He was delighted to have Erik accept him as an adventurous companion. "As you say, sir. As you say!"

Acting as if they were drunk with their triumphs, the two animals swaggered from the room. Defiantly, they walked up the very center of the incline instead of slinking along the wall. Ginger and Arletta could hear them quite clearly all the way to the first floor.

"I don't like any of this," said Ginger. "They're going to get us all in a terrible fix."

"What time does Mr. Fats usually come by?" asked Arletta.

Ginger looked worried. "Well, that's the trouble. He doesn't get out every night. Sometimes they take him right upstairs when the butcher shop closes."

Arletta moved a little closer to Ginger. "You know something? I'm beginning to like this city living. I've never met anyone like Erik the rat before. And that polite, cowardly opossum—I adore him. And, if I hadn't come here," she continued softly, "I would never have met you." She gazed at Ginger. "You know," she said shyly, "you never did tell me how *you* came to the hideaway."

"Oh, there isn't much to tell. I had always lived with my family in the Bronx, in a little neighborhood park. Humans used to come to sit on the benches in the sun and feed nuts and bread crumbs to the pigeons and the squirrels. It was very peaceful. Then one day men came along in big machines and started knocking down the trees. I couldn't believe my eyes! They were getting rid of the trees so they could build tall houses. When they started to knock down our tree, my family scattered. I soared down to the ground and hid in the pocket of a coat that I found in a parked car. It belonged to a lady who worked in The Mart. When she drove to the store and we were inside, I slipped out of the pocket and scurried down to the basement. My, but I was frightened! That's when I met Staten Island Fats. He showed me the hideaway, and I've lived here ever since."

"Don't you want to go back outdoors and live in a tree again?"

"Once in awhile I think about it, although I like it here."

Arletta sat silent for a moment. Then she said, "Let's always stay together, Ginger."

The rat and the opossum made a noisy return to the hideaway. Even from deep in her burrow Arletta could hear them coming down the incline to the subbasement. She came out to listen. Ginger swooped down and sat on top of the burrow.

"Here come the returning heroes," she said dryly, shaking her head as the two entered the room.

Norton looked at her. He seemed a little ashamed of himself for the way he had been acting.

"Ladies," he said anxiously, "surely you

must be hungry. Why don't you all go upstairs and get something to eat?"

"I'm not in the least bit hungry," snapped Ginger, "but I'll go anywhere just to get away from you two. Come along, Arletta."

Together they walked out of the room and cautiously made their way up to the top floor where they cast about halfheartedly for food.

Behind a counter Ginger found a broken jar of peanuts. "I wish they wouldn't salt these so much," she observed. "They make me thirsty. And it's such a long walk to the goldfish aquarium."

"Have some of these," said Arletta, rolling a dented can of unsalted pecans to her friend. "As for me, I think I'll sample this," she said, nibbling on a slice of salami.

The animals munched away, but it wasn't food that was on their minds.

"That Erik!" said Ginger. "He sure can act foolish when he sets out to do it." She cracked open a pecan and carefully put the shells in the waste can. "He really isn't mean, but sometimes that ratty instinct comes out."

"Does Norton always fall in with his plans?" asked Arletta, tidily trimming the rind from another slice of salami.

"Not like this time. But I suppose Norton has admired Erik secretly for quite awhile." The flying squirrel rummaged around in the waste bin. "Would you like some grapes? A cracker? Piece of apple?" she asked.

"No thanks," said Arletta, looking at her friend with affection. "Can you believe that we've known each other such a short time? I feel as though I've been close to you for years."

"And it was only yesterday," replied Ginger with a smile. The little animals sat in companionable silence for awhile. Finally Arletta sighed and said, "Well, I suppose we should go back to the hideaway. Maybe Mr. Fats has arrived."

Ginger brushed the last remaining pieces of nutshell from the soft fur on her breast. "Too early for Staten to come in, Arletta. If he manages to come at all tonight."

With a last look around, the two animals made their way down the flights of nonmoving escalator stairs. Even though it was dark and the store was absolutely deserted of humans, the animals took great care, just as Staten Island Fats had cautioned them. They came down along the baseboard of the incline and stopped and looked back as they reached the bottom; then their eyes searched up and down the hall before entering the hideaway. They came in so quietly they didn't rouse either Norton or Erik, who were sound asleep.

"I guess we might as well get some rest ourselves until Staten Island Fats gets here," whispered Ginger. "Good night, Arletta."

"Night, Ginger," replied the skunk, curling up in her hatbox, where she quickly fell asleep.

Chapter
8

Surprisingly, all the animals slept right through the rest of the night. It was the first sounds of activity in the store above that roused them. Arletta awoke and looked around to see if Staten Island Fats had arrived, but he was nowhere to be seen.

Ginger zoomed down from her box-top perch and landed next to Arletta. "Morning," she said pleasantly.

Erik, awake and alert, listened closely to the noises from above. "Store isn't opened yet. Just the store humans up there," he announced.

Norton came out from between the two barrels. "Guess Staten Island Fats couldn't make it last night," he drawled.

Erik cocked his head and looked at all of them. "I have an idea those trap-setters will come down to look at the traps before the store opens. I think it would be smart of us to move behind the wall for awhile."

Ginger gave the rat a disagreeable look. "Smart!" she said. "If you had been a little smarter yesterday, we wouldn't be hiding today."

"No time for arguing," said Arletta. "Let's tidy up and get out."

One by one the animals went out through the loose board into the darkness and made themselves as comfortable as they could along the pipe.

"Safest thing for all of us is to shut up from now on," rasped Erik.

"Look who's giving us advice on safety," snapped Ginger.

Nevertheless, the animals sat very still. There was no talking, not even whispering, among them. They felt a sense of danger in the quiet darkness. Arletta, the farthest along on the pipe, stirred uneasily. The hair prickled on her neck. She sniffed the air suspiciously. She was aware of motion behind her.

"Good morning," boomed a voice in her ear. Arletta leaped from the pipe in surprise. "What's the matter?" asked the deep voice. "It's I, Staten Island Fats." Suddenly he noticed that everyone was sitting on the pipe outside the room. "What's going on here?" he questioned. "Why is everyone out here? Is there trouble?"

"Nah," spoke up Erik breezily. "No trouble, Fats. But just the same, let's try to keep our voices low, eh?"

"Is that so?" asked Staten Island Fats icily. "All right, tell me all about it."

In an offhand manner Erik unfolded the story of his run-in with the workmen—how he had escaped from them and how they had set the traps in the hideaway. He couldn't restrain the bragging tone in his voice as he went on to describe the springing of the traps and the feast of cheese.

"And the reason we are sitting out here," broke in Ginger, "is that we expect those workmen to come down and inspect the traps before the store opens."

The huge cat was filled with fury. "You crazy fool!" he growled at the rat. "You nincompoop! You—you—you *rat*! So this is your idea of a big joke! And all the others have to suffer because you want to have a little laugh on the human race, eh? Well, Erik, the laughing isn't over, but *you* won't be the one to get the last laugh."

The big cat turned on Norton. "And you!" he snarled. "Whatever possessed you to—"

"*Sshh!*" warned Arletta. "I hear someone in our room!" The animals froze. The cat turned an ear in the direction of the hideaway. Sure enough, there were thumps coming from beyond the wall, and then the sound of voices.

Inside the room two young men in work clothes were stooping over the trap in the corner. They studied it and nodded to each other. Charlie sniffed the air. "Does it smell a little—a little *ratty* in here? Kind of *animally*?" he asked.

Bud inhaled sharply. "Well, it's not exactly a rose garden." He stood up and walked over to the other trap between the two barrels under the table and crouched over it.

"Same thing over here, Charlie. Cheese is gone."

Charlie walked around the room slowly, his

eyes on the ground. He stooped and peered into Arletta's box. Then he picked up the box with its open side down and shook it. He bent down and picked up something from the floor.

"Look at this, Bud," he said.

Bud walked over and peered at what Charlie held in his fingers. "What am I supposed to see, Charlie?"

"These hairs. Some are black. Some are white."

"You think they're rat hairs? Ain't they too long for rat hairs?"

"Yup," said Charlie. "Too long for rat hairs. But they are the hairs of *some* kind of animal. Maybe a cat. That's it! A black-and-white cat!"

"You suppose a cat ate the cheese? Cats don't eat cheese, do they?"

Charlie shook his head. "Nope. But there's a rat and some other kind of animal living in here. Must be." He stared thoughtfully at the hair in his fingers. "Why did we put those traps down here anyway?" he asked Bud. "Yesterday we saw a rat. Right? And today we find the cheese missing. Right? So who ate the cheese but was too quick for the trap? A smart rat. Right?"

"Right," said Bud.

"Now we find long black and white hairs. Too long for rat hairs. Right? But not too long for cat hairs. Right?"

"Right," said Bud.

"So now what do we have? A smart rat and a black-and-white cat waiting for him."

Charlie brushed Arletta's hair out of his hands. "Only one way to find out. I'll go get Major and put him in this room. If there's any kind of animal hanging around, Maje will find out for us."

"I wouldn't want to be a rat *or* a cat with that dog waiting for me," said Bud. He brushed the dust from his pants. "Come on, Charlie. Let's go. We've got a lot of work to do."

Leaving the traps where they were, the men left the room, their work boots echoing hollowly as they walked up the incline toward the basement.

Inside the wall, the animals sat quietly. They didn't make a sound. Then Ginger said, "I believe they have gone."

Erik said meekly, "Since I started all this, I'll go in and look around. Excuse me, Ginger, let me pass."

The rat pushed on the loose wallboard and

wiggled through. He sniffed at the air as his little eyes inspected the hideaway; then he scuttled over to the doorway and looked up and down the dark corridor. He even ventured out into the hallway before going back to the wallboard.

"No one in sight," he called softly. "It's safe to come in."

Chapter
9

The animals filed quietly back into the hideaway. Although they couldn't understand human conversation, the tone of the workmen's voices had upset them. Staten Island Fats prowled around the room. He paused before the trap in the corner and looked thoughtfully at it.

The others watched him uneasily. Norton felt quite ashamed for the part he had played in putting them in this fix. If only he had had the sense to think it through and the courage to tell Erik to leave the traps alone. The men would have come back, seen the cheese, and thought that no animals lived down in the subbasement. But it was too late now.

Arletta broke the silence. "Well, Mr. Fats, what do you make of it?"

The huge cat looked at her, then at all the other animals, one by one.

"Make of it?" he replied finally. "We're in trouble, that's what I make of it. Trouble. We are going to have to get out of here." He paced around the room, deep in thought. "Those workmen haven't given up; I'm sure of it. They're making other plans. And we'd better not wait too long to find out what they are."

"What should we do?" asked Arletta.

Without answering, the huge cat continued his prowl around the room; he stopped to study the long hair of the skunk that had been brushed onto the floor. He sniffed, shook his enormous head, and continued his pacing. In the middle of the room he stopped and sat down on his haunches.

"My friends," he began formally, "the time has come to abandon this hideaway. We must either find a new hideaway, or we must say good-bye to each other and go our separate ways. I already *have* a home, but if you would like to stay in the vicinity, I'll help you resettle."

"And what would be your advice, sir, if I

may inquire?'' asked Norton politely.

"My suggestion would be to find another good spot near here,'' said Staten Island Fats.

"I agree. I like the neighborhood,'' said Erik, trying to make himself as pleasant as possible.

"That's how I feel,'' said Norton.

"Well,'' said Arletta in a firm voice, "I've had enough of this indoor city life. I want to find some way to get back to the country.''

"Of course, my dear,'' said the big cat understandingly. "We will try to devise a plan to smuggle you out of the city.'' He looked at Ginger. "What about you, child?''

The little flying squirrel cocked her head toward the skunk. "I think I'll string along with Arletta. We've become quite attached to each other.''

"Very well,'' the cat said briskly. "One destination for the two of you shouldn't be too difficult to manage.''

He turned to the opossum and the rat. "Well, gentlemen, we are faced with the need for strategy and action,'' he said. "The situation is so crucial I feel obliged to take the day off from my job at the butcher shop.''

"Oh, dear!" exclaimed Arletta. "Won't that be bad for you? I wouldn't want you to get in trouble at home just for our sake. We'll make out somehow," said Arletta optimistically.

"Don't worry your pretty little black-and-white head over me, my dear," he said with a smile. "I've earned a day off. Anyway, they're always glad to see me whenever I do show up."

He signaled the animals to come closer so that he could explain his plans quietly.

"We have two very important things to do," he began. "First, we must search for a new hide-away, and second, we must get the ladies out of here and back to the country. I'd like to hear your ideas first; then I've got a few suggestions of my own."

"Let's hear your ideas first, Fats," said Erik. "Mine haven't been so great lately," he added sourly.

"Very well," said the cat. "I think Erik and I should search for a new place to live. Erik is small and fast, and tough enough to take care of himself. As for me, nobody bothers with a cat. And since I'm well-known in the neighborhood, I can roam without arousing suspicion."

He turned to Norton. "Your job may be a

little more dangerous. But it will have to be done because we must get Arletta and Ginger safely out to the country."

The opossum shuddered but said gallantly, "Whatever you say, sir. Just tell me what I must do."

"In a short while, you will go to the loading platform in back of the store. Pick out a hiding place where you can watch the delivery trucks as they are loaded. It will be up to you to find which truck makes deliveries to the suburbs so that we can get Arletta and Ginger on it."

"A fine plan, sir! But how can I tell which truck goes to the country and which delivers to the city?"

"You will have to use good judgment, Norton," said the cat. "Didn't you say you grew up in the country? Maybe you'll be able to recognize some of the things that go into the trucks. Things that country people would buy this time of year, like rakes for leaves, fertilizer for lawns, or other supplies people use to prepare for cold weather." He looked at the opossum very earnestly. "It will be terribly important that you decide on the right truck, Norton," he said softly. "Make sure."

"I will do my best," said the opossum

stoically. "And sir, let me say how sorry I am for my part in yesterday's foolishness. If I had only had the sense to think it through—"

The rat interrupted him. "Bah! It's all my fault for forcing you. Anyway, that's all water into the sewer now. Let's forget it."

"Correct," said Staten Island Fats. "There are more important things to think about at the moment." He looked at the opossum. "Norton, I think you should start for the loading area before the store opens. Go now, before anyone turns up, and find yourself a good hiding place. Somewhere where you can see without being seen. You should be able to find the right truck for the ladies."

"Very good, sir!" Norton nodded to the skunk and the squirrel as if to say, you can depend on me, and slipped through the open door into the corridor.

"Our blessings go with him," said the big cat as the animals listened to Norton scurrying away along the hall. "I do hope he makes it all right."

"Aah, don't worry about Nort," said Erik. "He feels so bad about yesterday that he'll be extra careful from now on."

The cat turned his orange eyes on the rat.

"Now, Erik. We should begin looking for a new hideaway. I will search along the streets. You do the inside work. You know what to look for— a place with several safe exits and entrances that also has food and water nearby—a place humans are not likely to visit often." He paused, lost in thought. "I have in mind a warehouse, or another department store."

He turned his attention to Ginger and Arletta. "I believe it would be best if you ladies spent the day outside this room, sitting on the pipe." He smiled encouragingly. "I know it won't be comfortable, but we mustn't take any chances today, especially with you ladies."

He walked with the two little animals toward the loose wallboard. "You two have the hardest job of all, for you may have to sit outside for hours without making a sound. And remember, no matter what happens in this room, do not become panicky. If you feel threatened, just retreat along the pipe as far as the outside wall. You will be safe, I'm sure."

He paused and gazed affectionately from one to the other. "Farewell, Ginger. I will miss you. And Arletta, I'm sorry you weren't with us longer. I hope you both find happiness wherever you go."

Erik scuttled over. "Good-bye, good-bye. Sorry about the mess I got you into."

"Good-bye, rat," said Ginger. "Keep away from the traps."

"So long, Erik," said Arletta as she let her gaze wander around the room and was surprised at the fondness she felt for it. It made her think that once again she was leaving home.

"I will check with you as soon as I can," Staten Island Fats told the two animals. "There is much work to be done before this day is over."

Quietly Arletta and Ginger slipped through the loose wallboard and settled themselves as comfortably as they could on the pipe. They would have loved to discuss the events of the last few hours, but they knew they couldn't. It was indeed going to be a long day.

Chapter
10

Carefully Norton walked up the incline on his way to the loading platform. His mind was filled with the importance of his assignment. He alone was responsible for finding safe transportation for his friends. Then he began to wonder what would happen to him if he got caught. The opossum shuddered at the thought, for Norton liked the life he led. He enjoyed the cozy comforts of the hideaway and took pleasure in his companions. He had great admiration for Staten Island Fats, and the ladies were a special delight to him. Even Erik was turning out to be a good sort of fellow, although his manners were appalling. All things considered, life in the hideaway was pleasant and easy. It saddened Norton to think they were all leaving it.

This is no time for sentimental thoughts, Norton told himself; I must keep my mind on this job. He stopped and craned his neck to look behind him and peer around on all sides. There was nothing to be seen. Slowly and noiselessly he made his way up the incline.

At the top, he poked his head around the corner, then scurried along the empty aisles leading to the back of the basement. Again he looked around carefully. Still there was no one in sight. At the back wall was a metal package chute like a child's slide. It was used to send small packages out to the loading platform near the trucks. Norton hoisted himself onto the chute and let go. Down he slid and out he went through the little door, which clicked shut behind him.

He landed outside on a corner of the empty loading platform. It was too early for anyone from the store to be there. Within a few minutes he found a safe vantage point between two garbage cans at the entrance to the alley. Hungrily he looked at one of the garbage cans. The lid was loose, and he thought about peeking to see if there was a snack inside. Firmly he put the thought out of his mind. This was no time to disobey orders or to look for trouble.

Norton settled down between the garbage cans. It was a perfect spot. He could clearly see the three trucks that were lined up against the platform, and he would be able to tell what packages were being loaded into each of them. With a drawn-out sigh of satisfaction, the opossum readied himself for the long hours ahead.

Erik and Staten Island Fats left The Mart together through the hole behind the standpipe. It was still dark outside, and the two stayed close to each other. Even as they hurried along they kept a sharp watch for good hideaway locations. When they reached the corner of the second block, Staten Island Fats looked down the side street and saw a row of houses and small stores. Some of them were boarded up and appeared deserted.

"This street looks promising, Erik," said the big cat. "Why don't you investigate while I scout the rest of the neighborhood. Stay out of sight. I'll come by later, and we'll talk things over."

"Right," said the rat. "Good luck, Fats."

The big cat padded away, and Erik scuttled around to the back of the first house. He wriggled

through a broken window into the cellar. It smelled unpleasantly musty. The walls were damp and the paint had peeled away in long, limp strips. In one corner of the ceiling a leaky waterpipe dripped steadily. It was the kind of old house that Erik had a taste for, but he knew that Staten Island Fats would loathe it. And it certainly was no place for ladies. He left it and scurried over to the next house.

This one seemed to be in much better shape. The cellar was large and dry and cluttered with old trunks and piles of books and broken furniture, offering a fine choice of hiding places. Erik slipped through a small hole in the floor to check on the condition of the walls. He picked his way through bits of broken plaster, looking for emergency exits. His path was blocked by a large piece of wood wedged into the wall. He tried to get around it by hoisting himself onto a wooden lath. It was rotten and dry. Suddenly, with a sharp snap, it gave way under the rat's weight. A torrent of loose plaster showered down on Erik with a deafening roar. Everything went black, and for a moment Erik thought he was dead. He wriggled and pushed and jerked. Finally, after a desperate struggle, he yanked himself free. Forcing himself to be calm, Erik studied his situation. He decided he was in terrible trouble. One of his back legs hurt very badly. The hole he had come through was packed solid with fallen plaster. The large piece of wood still blocked the way in front of him. Erik realized he would have to gnaw and dig his way out if he was to reach the hole he had come in through. It would take a long time. He'd be lucky to get out of this mess alive.

The strain was beginning to tell on Arletta and Ginger. They had been huddling on the pipe for what seemed like hours. Even though the store hadn't opened yet, they didn't feel it was safe to talk. The air that seeped in from the outside was chilling and damp. Arletta shivered and wrapped her tail more snugly around herself. Her eyes met Ginger's, and there was no happiness in the glance.

Suddenly Arletta heard sounds from within the room, and all her senses were alerted. Ginger had heard them too. She turned toward Arletta questioningly.

They sat perfectly still and watched in terror as the loose wallboard began to jiggle. Arletta jerked her head at Ginger to indicate that they should retreat along the pipe. A voice whispered to them. "Don't move! It's me, Nor-

ton." A wave of relief came over Arletta as she and Ginger watched the opossum push through the wallboard and climb onto the pipe. He was soaking wet and looked quite bedraggled.

"Brrr!" he shivered. "It's raining outside. How I hate the rain."

"What are you doing here, Norton?" asked Arletta in surprise. "You aren't supposed to come back until much later."

"I know," said the opossum. "But something tells me to get you two out of here now. This minute. Please, please take my word for it!" he pleaded.

"But what about Mr. Fats?" asked Arletta. "His instructions were for us to wait, remember?"

"Yes, indeed, ma'am, I know. I also know this feeling I have. It tells me that if you don't leave here right away something awful is going to happen. So come on, ladies."

Arletta looked at Ginger. "What do you think?" she asked.

Ginger considered the situation at some length. Finally she said, "I believe in Norton's instinct. We ought to go with him. Staten Island Fats would agree with that."

"Then that settles it," said Arletta.

"Let's hurry, ladies," said the opossum. "Now here is what we're going to do. We'll sneak along to the rear of the bargain-basement floor. I didn't see anyone down there, but we will have to be careful. There's a package slide on the back wall that will shoot us out of the building right to the loading platform. I have a safe spot picked out between two garbage cans where we can see everything without being seen. After we pick out the truck going to the country, I will put my secret plan into action."

"Secret plan? What secret plan?" asked Ginger.

"I hope it won't be dangerous for you?" asked Arletta worriedly.

"Now, now, ladies. Don't you fret over me," said the opossum with his brave new smile. "Come, follow me, and be very careful. Remember, it's raining outside."

Chapter

11

The animals hurried along the platform and through the pouring rain to Norton's post between the garbage cans. Only a few minutes later, after they had settled as comfortably as possible behind the cans close to the wall, The Mart began to come alive. Clerks and cashiers and stockroom boys and floor managers arrived at the doors, shaking their umbrellas and whipping the rain from their hats. One of the workmen led a large German police dog on a leather leash. "Come on, Major," he said, "we've got work to do. Soon as I change my clothes we'll get hold of Bud. Then you can catch a rat and a cat for us. You'll have some fun, let me tell you."

The dog stood obediently by his master, shaking the water off his tan coat as Charlie changed into his work clothes. He was soon joined by his friend Bud.

"Miserable day, ain't it, Charlie, with the rain and all," he greeted his partner.

"Maje and I are going to brighten it up for you, Bud. We're going to hunt down those smart-aleck animals this morning."

They led the police dog down the incline and into the deserted hideaway. Major sniffed his way around the room, running this way and that. The hair on the back of his neck stood out stiff with excitement. He spent a long time snuffling in Erik's favorite corner. Then he sniffed his way slowly under the table. Going along the wall, he stopped suddenly in front of the loose wallboard. His ears shot up. He growled and he whined and he pawed at the loose board. It gave a little.

"Say! Look at that, Bud!" exclaimed Charlie excitedly. "Did you see it move?"

The dog caught the fever in his master's voice. He barked and scratched wildly at the board. Charlie hurried over and bent down to examine it. "Well, I'll be doggoned!" he cried out. "So this is where they were hiding!" He tugged at the loose board and pulled it toward himself as hard as he could. "Look in there, Bud."

Bud kneeled down and peered into the space behind the wall. "Nothing in here but a big pipe. It runs a couple of feet to the outside of the building. It's the standpipe."

He scrunched down a little farther to get a better look. "Seems like there's a space out near where the pipe comes in. A big crack or something behind the pipe."

"Let's get out there and take a look," Charlie said. He turned to the dog. "Maje, you stay right here. Stay. Catch anything that comes through."

Not even stopping to put on their raincoats, the men rushed outside the store and around to the standpipe. Charlie bent down and put his hand behind the pipe. "Wow! What a crack! So that's how those pesky animals went in and out of the store. We'll fix them, all right!"

He turned to his friend. "We've got to plaster the hole over on this side and nail that loose board inside. That will be the end of that!" he said triumphantly.

Around at the back of the store the little animals, hunched together in the rain and the cold, had no idea of how close they had come to a dreadful end. They stared through the rain and the grayness of the morning at the three trucks backed against the platform, their rear doors swung wide open to receive the day's parcels, crates, boxes, and packages. Patiently, the animals waited for the store to open and the packages to start coming to the platform for sorting.

One by one the drivers of the trucks straggled out, their caps pulled low over their faces and their necks hunched into the collars of their raincoats. They spoke a word or two of greeting to one another and waited inside their trucks for the packages to arrive.

Soon little boxes and packages began to whoosh out the chute door to be picked up and sorted by a checking clerk. Larger packages were brought to the platform by other clerks or were carted out on handtrucks.

The animals paid close attention to everything that went into the trucks. They were straining to see something they could recognize as being used in the country, but most of the packages were wrapped. The animals had little chance to identify any of the items. Once, when a long parcel came out, Arletta said, "That could be a rake! Let's watch where they put it."

"It could also be a broom," Ginger said gloomily.

"Or a shotgun," said Norton, flinching at the thought.

The animals watched. They could not recognize a thing. They began to get discouraged.

Suddenly Arletta noticed something familiar. "Look!" she exclaimed. "I know I've seen that!"

The animals looked at a large white bag being carried by one of the clerks. GREEN THUMB FERTILIZER was written on the bag in green letters, and under the letters was a circle with a picture of a fist with a large green thumb sticking up.

"I've seen men putting that on lawns all over my neighborhood!" whispered Arletta excitedly. "I *know* they use that in the country."

"Keep your eyes open, everybody!" urged Ginger. "Make sure you see where he puts it!"

The boy lowered the bag down in the middle of the platform.

"Oh, no!" moaned Arletta. "He isn't putting it into *any* truck!"

"He will, ma'am," said Norton soothingly.

The boy reached into his pocket for a handkerchief and blew his nose loudly, then picked up the bag of fertilizer.

"Watch carefully!" implored Arletta.

They stared hard at the boy as he walked along the platform past the first truck and past the second. He handed the bag to the driver of the third truck. The driver said something that made the boy laugh, then disappeared inside the truck with the bag.

"That's the one!" said Arletta joyfully. "That's the truck for us, Ginger! But how are we going to get inside it without being seen?" asked Arletta.

"Ah!" said Norton. "I have a plan all worked out."

"I hope this plan is better than the one you had with the rat," said Ginger.

"If you please, ma'am. Allow me to explain." Norton stroked his whiskers nervously. Arletta noticed that his paws were trembling. "In a minute I will stroll out onto the platform and attract the attention of the drivers and clerks. When they see me, they will all try to catch me. But I will not let them. I'll lead them up and down the platform and then finally out into the street. When I do, you two scurry into the truck and hide. By that time I will have made my escape." He smiled at them weakly.

The two animals stared at him in horror.

"No, no, Norton!" cried Arletta. "It's much too dangerous! What if they catch you? Why, they might even—they might kill you!"

"She's right, Norton," said Ginger. "Don't give yourself up for us. We'll find a way to get into the truck. You'll see."

The gentlemanly opossum ignored their protests. "Get ready, ladies. I'm about to step out. And remember, when you run for the truck, don't look back. I will be all right." In spite of his brave words Norton looked frightened. "Here I go, ladies! Good luck to you!"

Shaking with nervousness, the opossum stepped out in the rain and walked quite close to the trucks. No one paid any attention to him. He strolled back and forth, his confidence returning to him. Still no one noticed him. Finally, with a newborn spirit, he called out, "All right, gentlemen! Here I am. Come and get me if you can!" The words came out of his throat sounding like *"Skreenk! Skreenk!"*

The truck drivers and the clerks stopped what they were doing and turned toward the strange sound. They stood open-mouthed at the sight of the opossum. Finally one driver pointed at Norton and exclaimed, "Criminy! Looka the size of that rat!"

"That's no rat," said a clerk. "It's a weasel."

"Nah!" said a package carrier. "It's a raccoon!"

"A beaver!"

"A woodchuck!"

"Some sort of a wild cat!"

Norton began to enjoy himself. *"Skree skrink skree!"* he called.

One of the clerks, a serious-looking young man, came out on the platform with a package in his hands. He looked at Norton and said, "Good heavens! A *Didelphis virginiana!*"

The drivers stared at him.

"That's a Virginia opossum," he continued. "A fine example of an American marsupial, chiefly nocturnal and largely arboreal. I wonder what it is doing here."

One of the truck drivers said, "Who cares *what* he's doing here. Let's get him!" He jumped down from the platform and started to waddle toward Norton. The other men straggled along behind him.

Norton looked over his shoulder at the garbage cans; then he slowly loped toward the farthest corner of the loading area. The men quickly took up the chase.

Norton began to run faster, toward the opening of the driveway where the trucks turned in from the street. Hooting and yelling, the men stamped after him. At the entrance to the street, Norton stopped short and quickly changed his course. The men behind him piled into each other. A few were knocked off their feet, landing with grunts and curses. Laughing to himself, Norton scurried around them and pranced off in exactly the opposite direction, toward the trucks.

"*Skrine! Skrine!*" he called. "Hurry up! Hurry up!"

The men unscrambled themselves and set out after him again. Norton dashed under the middle truck and sat down, his eyes dancing with pleasure. He was beginning to have a marvelous time. His pursuers gathered around the truck, and several got down on their hands and knees in puddles of rainwater to look at the opossum. Norton pretended to yawn.

Then unexpectedly he shot out from under the truck, scrambled over the back of one man who was bent over to watch him, and leaped out into the open. It took his chasers a few minutes to collect themselves and start after him again. Norton headed for the garbage cans. "Here's your chance, ladies!" he shouted as he sped by. Out into the street he ran, the men in splashing pursuit.

Ginger peered out from behind the cans. "Now!" she called to Arletta. "Let's fly for it!"

They raced into the driving rain, heading straight for the end truck, the one that would take them to the country. But just as they neared the line of trucks, Ginger heard a noise behind her. She cast a quick look over her shoulder. A young clerk with a big package had just emerged from the back of the store and was crossing the loading platform.

"Quick, Arletta!" she called. "In here for now!" They dove into the middle truck and scrambled behind two large cartons just as the boy came into view.

"Whew!" gasped Ginger. "A narrow escape! But we're in the wrong truck!"

"First things first," said Arletta. "First we save our lives, *then* we worry about the right truck. Let's just wait here and see what happens."

They huddled together behind the boxes, catching their breath and waiting for the oppor-

tunity to get into the right truck. Their chances to scoot out grew dimmer and dimmer as more and more packages were carried onto the platform and loaded into the trucks. Arletta and Ginger listened to the rattlings and the thumpings and watched the pile of boxes and cartons between them and the back of the truck grow higher and higher.

"Getting pretty crowded in here," observed Arletta. She peered out from behind her carton and saw another load coming through the doorway. She turned to Ginger. "I hate to say it, my friend, but we may not be able to get out of here."

"Not get out!" exclaimed Ginger. "After all our hard work! And Norton's bravery! What will we do?"

"Oh, well!" said Arletta trying to sound cheerful. "We'll just go along for the ride. The driver's got to stop *somewhere*. Lots of places, in fact. We'll have a long time to decide what's best for us."

Suddenly they heard the sounds of cheering and laughter in the distance. They looked at each other in horror.

"Norton!" whispered Arletta.

The shouts and the laughter grew louder.

"I'm going to peek out," said Arletta.

"Please be careful!" advised the squirrel.

Cautiously Arletta worked her way between the packages to the tail end of the truck and poked out her head. The sound of cheering was coming from the street where the drivers and the clerks had been chasing Norton. They were laughing and joking among themselves as they surged back toward the store. Two of them carried a closed cardboard carton. Arletta pulled her head in and slowly picked her way back to Ginger.

"I'm afraid it's bad news," she said softly.

"Norton?"

Arletta nodded.

"Is he—is he all right?" asked Ginger in a small voice.

"There was no way to tell. The men were carrying a box. I guess Norton was in it."

The animals felt very unhappy. For once in her life Arletta could not see the bright side. She turned away from the squirrel as she fought back her tears.

"They are loading up fast. I think I'll watch for our last chance to get out of here," said Ginger.

Huddled forlornly behind a carton, Arletta did not even lift her head. "I don't care. I don't care what happens to me now. Poor Norton. He did it for us.''

With a clanking, crashing noise, the gate doors of the truck slammed shut. The motor roared. The truck began to move.

''We're off,'' said Ginger.

Arletta didn't answer.

Chapter
12

After he left Erik at the row of old houses, Staten Island Fats decided to examine every street in the several blocks around The Mart. He knew the task would take him a long time, but he didn't mind. He wanted to see for himself all the possibilities for another hideaway in the neighborhood. Even with Arletta and Ginger gone, he still had to think of Norton and Erik. And what if the ladies failed to make good their getaway? They would need a decent place to come back to.

The big cat took his time. With a careful eye, he studied each house and store on every block. Those he considered suitable prospects would be investigated later from within by Erik.

When he was about halfway through his job, the rain began to fall, gently at first, but soon in hard cold sheets. Staten Island Fats was soaked right through his long gray fur, but he was determined to finish his undertaking. He had arrived at the block facing the rear entrance to The Mart. Staten Island Fats was across the street when a chorus of hoots and shouts erupted from the driveway. Moving quickly, he got to a spot where he could see what was going on. His eyes met a chilling sight. Out of the driveway skittered Norton running as hard as he could, fear showing in his face. Pounding along behind him in hot pursuit was a gang of laughing, yelling men. As the cat turned his head to follow the chase, his eye caught another tense scene.

From behind two garbage cans raced Arletta and Ginger heading up the incline to the loading platform. The cat watched them as they flew across the platform toward the trucks and disappeared from sight. A surge of relief came over the cat. They made it! Quickly he turned his attention back to the chase. Norton was still on the loose, wheeling this way, turning that way. But it was sickeningly clear to the cat that Norton would be caught. And as he watched, a pair of hands shot out and grabbed the opossum

100

by the scruff of his neck and held him up, to the cheers of the pursuers. One of the men handed over a large carton, and Norton was dumped into it. Amid whistles and cries of victory, the men carried the box through the rear entrance into the store.

With an aching sadness, Staten Island Fats turned away and padded off in search of Erik.

Chapter
13

Erik was in terrible pain. His back leg, swollen to twice its size, throbbed and ached. His body felt hot. His jaws hurt as he gnawed his way through the plaster and wood that had fallen all around him. Every once in awhile the rat would feel as if a sheet of red were coming down before his eyes, and he would faint. He felt very weak.

All through the morning he had been biting and chewing, fighting to find a way out of his trap. The work was very hard, and he was forced to take longer and longer rests.

Erik had just about decided that all his efforts were useless when his long nose poked through the pile of debris. Not six feet ahead of him was the hole in the wall through which he had entered. Slowly he crawled toward it, and with great care he wriggled through the wall and into the cellar.

In a few minutes he was outdoors. The rat hunched himself against a wall in the alley behind the building and let the rain pour down on his aching body. It felt grand. He hobbled to a rain puddle and drank until his stomach could hold no more. Feeling refreshed, he set off to find Staten Island Fats.

He slunk along close to the buildings as he started on his painful trip. Erik was grateful that the day was gloomy. His gray fur blended so perfectly with the grayness of the day that he almost disappeared from sight. Not many humans were out on the streets this miserable day. Just as well, thought Erik, as he limped along dragging his swollen leg. He hoped that all hungry cats were staying indoors too. In his condition, he wouldn't stand much of a chance even against a small one.

Just as he was thinking that unwelcome thought, a huge cat came into view. Erik pressed against the building and bared his teeth, preparing for what he believed would be his last fight. Then he relaxed. The cat was Staten Island Fats.

"Am I glad to see *you*!" sighed the rat in relief.

"Erik!" exclaimed Staten Island Fats. "I've been searching near and far for you. What in the world happened?"

"A wall fell on me. But I'm all right. More important is what's happened to the others. Do you know?" The rat looked at the cat with unusual concern.

"Yes. I have good news and bad. I'm almost certain that Arletta and Ginger got away all right. I saw them run along the loading platform toward the trucks and then they disappeared. I feel sure they made it into one of the trucks."

"That's the good news. I guess the bad news is about Norton?"

Staten Island Fats looked unhappy. "Norton was captured. Some men put him in a box and carried him away."

Both animals were silent for awhile. Then Staten Island Fats said, "You look terrible. We'd better take care of you right away." He thought for a few seconds and then said, "We'll go back to the butcher shop. There's a little hideout in the cellar. I'll get you something to eat and tell you all about the others. Come along."

The cat and the rat made a strange pair as

they plodded along in the rain, one behind the other. As they neared The Mart the cat turned to Erik. "Hide yourself for a few minutes. I'm going to snoop around outside the store and see what else I can find out."

Erik dragged himself under a parked car, and Staten Island Fats scampered across the street to the front of The Mart. As he approached the brass standpipe he noticed that the crack behind it had been sealed. He turned into the driveway to the loading area. All the trucks were gone.

The cat went back to where Erik was waiting. "Well, the delivery trucks are gone, and I guess Arletta and Ginger are on one of them. I just don't know anything more about Norton."

They continued on their way to the butcher shop. When they reached it, Staten Island Fats motioned to a broken pane of glass behind the iron bars of a cellar window. "In here," he said. "Hurry, please." He picked his way through, the rat close behind him. The cat led the way to a spot behind a hot water tank in the corner. "Make yourself comfortable," he said, "while I go up and get you something to eat. Would you rather have lamb or chicken?"

"Anything," gasped Erik, "as long as it's food."

Later on, while Erik gnawed on a duck wing, they talked over the events of the morning.

The big cat's face turned thoughtful. "Now, Erik, what are we going to do about you? I would gladly put you up here in the cellar, but it gets inspected quite often. And the inspectors pay special attention to fellows like you," he said with a sad smile.

"Don't worry about me, Fats. I'll be all right."

"Right now you aren't," replied the cat. "I would like to know that you are located some place where you'll be taken care of."

Erik nibbled the last sliver of meat from the duck wing. "I've got it all figured out, Fats," he said. "I'm going to live with my brother on his boat. There's plenty to eat, and the sea air will be good for me in my condition."

"His boat!" exclaimed the big cat in surprise. "What kind of boat?"

"Well, my brother calls it the *Leftover*. It's not actually a boat," Erik admitted sheepishly. "It's a garbage scow. He's lived on it for years. Every night it ties up at the dock, loads up, and in the morning starts off on a long, pleasant trip down the river and out to sea. It's a marvelous voyage. I took it once with him."

"Why didn't you stay on it?"

"It's a dull life, Fats." The rat moved his swollen leg tenderly. "But I think I've had enough excitement to last me for awhile."

The big cat looked worried. "Do you think you can find your way to the river?"

"Oh, I'll make it all right. Don't worry about *that*. If you'll be good enough to let me stay here until dark, I'll start out then."

"Of course, Erik. But be careful."

All through the day the rat rested and slept, waking only to eat the nourishing morsels Staten Island Fats brought from the shop. When it was time to go, he felt greatly refreshed. Staten Island Fats walked with him to the window. The rat turned to his friend for the last time. "Goodbye, Fats," he said. "It was a pleasure knowing a cat like you."

Without another word, he painfully hoisted himself up and out through the window. Hours later, exhausted, he crawled onto the garbage scow in search of his brother.

"Erik!" greeted his brother, a much older and grayer rat. "Goodness, you look awful! Let me take you to my quarters. You can tell me what's happened after you have some rest. Glad to have you aboard though."

With a long sigh of relief, Erik followed his brother to the hiding place that was to be his new home.

I don't care, thought Norton. I really don't care what they do to me now. As long as Arletta and Ginger are safe. And I do hope they are. He shifted around uncomfortably in the cardboard box. Let them kill me if they want to. What do I care?

In spite of his brave talk, the Virginia opossum was frightened. Ever since the men from The Mart had caught him and put him in the cardboard box, he had felt in his bones that he was doomed. Only once did someone open the box to have a look at him. He had been lifted out and examined, then put back in the box and loaded into a truck.

As Norton was thinking his worrisome thoughts the truck stopped. The back doors were swung open and Norton's box was lifted out. He heard the scraping of a door and knew he was being carried inside a building. Suddenly the box opened, and the opossum felt the pressure of human hands. Norton cringed in fear, but the hands lifted him out carefully and put him down gently on a long table. A man in a white coat looked at the frightened opossum and spoke quietly. "Now, now, young fellow, take it easy. Everything will be all right. I'm just going to look you over."

He ran his fingers over Norton's fur, lifted the animal's lips and examined his teeth, pinched open his mouth, and looked into his throat. Then he looked into the opossum's eyes and ears with a little light. "Fine, just fine," he murmured soothingly. He put a few drops of medicine on a piece of bread and held it in front of Norton's nose. The opossum sniffed at it suspiciously then snapped it up. Norton was hungry.

"All right, my friend," said the man in the white coat, "away you go."

Another man, in a green uniform, picked up Norton and carried him off in his arms. Norton was beginning to feel pretty good about things. Maybe they weren't going to kill him after all! The man took him into a dim room and unlocked the door of what looked like a little glass den. Gently he put Norton inside. Norton looked around the den. There was straw on the floor and a small cave he could go into whenever he wanted a little snooze. In a corner of the den were two bowls for food and water. Above his cave Norton spied a little dead tree he could climb onto.

The opossum strolled around his new home. It was certainly cozy. Then he looked through the glass wall and saw that there were many little dens like his lined up on both sides of the room. He craned his neck to see if he had any neighbors. As his eyes became accustomed to the dim light he could see that each little glass den had an animal in it. Ah! thought the opossum, this must be a zoo! I'm saved! I'm going to live happily ever after in a *zoo*, with not a worry in the world! He ambled into his cave, sniffed a few times, turned around once or twice, and finally lay down in the corner. He lowered his head onto his paws and, with a huge sigh of contentment, fell into a peaceful sleep.

Norton was awakened from his pleasant nap by a rattling sound in his den. He yawned, stretched, and then stepped out of his cave to see what the racket was all about. In his feeding bowl was a good-sized chunk of meat and two apples. The man in the green uniform who had carried him to his den stood outside and looked at him affectionately for a few seconds, then walked to the next den. He poked some food in through the barred top of the den and walked on.

Norton looked at his neighbor in the little cage to his right. It was another opossum, but one with stripes! Norton scooped up an apple and strolled over toward the glass wall which separated him from his neighbor.

"Good day, sir!" he called. "May I introduce myself? My name is Norton, and I'm an opossum from Virginia."

"Pleasure to know you," acknowledged his neighbor. "I am Luma, a striped opossum from the jungles of New Guinea. I'm sure you will enjoy it here in the Bronx Zoo."

Norton munched on his apple. "Delighted with it already. The food seems to be very good."

"Yes," said his neighbor, "and the service is excellent—when you consider the fact that there are about three thousand of us animals here."

"Amazing!" declared Norton.

"Indeed," continued the striped opossum, "you are in grand company here. We are among the finest and most unusual animals in the world. At our zoo there are African dingos, gorillas from mountains *and* lowlands, and a whole family of okapi which, as you undoubtedly know, are relatives of the giraffe."

"Of course, sir!" said Norton. He finished his apple. "If you will excuse me, I'd like to acquaint myself with my other next-door neighbor." The animals nodded politely to each other, and Norton walked to the other side of his den and looked through the glass wall. There he saw a breathtaking sight. In the cage was the most ravishing creature he had ever laid eyes on.

"How do you do," he said softly. "I'm Norton."

"*Buenos días, señor*," said his neighbor. "My name is Juanita, and I am a yapok from South America."

"Yapok?" asked Norton.

"*Sí*," replied Juanita, "that is to say, a water opossum." She lowered her head shyly. "They say yapoks are the most beautiful of all opossums. No offense meant," she said to Norton.

"And no offense taken, ma'am! None at all!" He stared at her. "I would say that yapoks are the most beautiful of *all* creatures."

"*Gracias, señor*. Thank you, but it is not so. I understand that, in the bird house at our zoo, you will find the rare and lovely moss-throated bellbird. Also the regal Congo peacocks. They are so lovely to look at."

"I'm sure they can't hold a candle to you,

ma'am," said Norton gallantly. "May I offer you an apple?"

The water opossum shook her head shyly.

Norton bit into his second apple, chewed away for awhile, and then asked, "Tell me, Juanita, why is it so dim in here? Why aren't there more lights on?"

"Because it is supposed to be nighttime in this room right now."

"Nighttime?" asked Norton. "Why is that, ma'am?"

"You see, almost all of us here in the Small Mammal House are night animals. We like to be active during the night and sleep through the day, but the humans who visit the zoo like to see us move around instead of sleep. So the zoo people turn day into night in this room. They leave on only a few soft, red lights during the day to make us think it is night so that we can go about our business. After visiting hours they turn on bright lights, and we think it is daytime and go to sleep." She smiled a little. "The zoo people think we don't know the difference," she said.

"Mighty smart humans, these zoo people," observed Norton.

"And they are kind, too," added Juanita.

"Well," said Norton, "I've only been here a short time, and already I think it's wonderful. And I'm going to *love* being right next door to you, ma'am." He looked around contentedly. "If Arletta and Ginger and the others could only see me now," he sighed with pleasure.

Chapter 14

Inside the dark truck, Arletta and Ginger didn't find much to say to each other. It would have been difficult in any case to talk above the roar of the motor and the squeaks and thumps of the jiggling freight. But their gloomy thoughts about Norton depressed them and kept them quiet.

After what seemed like a very long ride, the truck came to a stop and the driver turned off the motor.

"I think the driver is making his first delivery," whispered Ginger to Arletta. "I'm going to wriggle close to the door. When he opens it, I'll be able to see what it's like out there. You stay here until I call you.''

Ginger disappeared between a wide paper-wrapped parcel and a long skinny box. Arletta stayed between the two cartons.

Sure enough, the driver swung open the back doors and hopped into the truck. He riffled through his delivery slips, then searched for the packages which went with them. Ginger had plenty of time to study the outdoors. The driver found his packages, jumped out of the truck, and slammed the gates shut.

In a few seconds Ginger was back with Arletta. ''Nothing but a city street out there,'' she said. ''Big buildings, gray pavement, lots of autos and trucks. Not many humans though. And it is raining harder than ever.''

Arletta didn't answer. Ginger looked at her sharply. After a few minutes of silence, the flying squirrel spoke.

''Listen to me, friend,'' she said softly, ''I can't stand to see you look so downcast. You *must* cheer up. I know you are thinking about Norton, and I am too. I really don't believe anything bad has happened to him. But if it did, there is nothing he would rather do than die a brave hero.''

Arletta lifted her head. "Of course you are right, Ginger. I'm sorry to be so gloomy. It's just that I can't bear the thought of anything bad happening to poor Norton. He was such a dear. And I do miss the others, too," she added. "But don't worry, Ginger. I'll behave better. I promise."

"Oh, that's all right," answered the squirrel. "But now," she went on briskly, "we must make our plans. We've got to face the possibility that we may never get to the country at all. So I think we should move as close as we can to the back door and be prepared to jump out at every stop. When the driver opens the door, we'll look the neighborhood over. If we think it's a nice one, we'll jump out and make a run for it."

The animals waited eagerly for the next stop. When the motor died down, they were ready. Arletta was crouched between two square boxes with enough room between them for her to dash out if she had to. Ginger was on top of the tallest stack of packages, hidden from view but in a fine position to scoot out.

While they waited, Arletta said, "For all we know, when the driver swings open that door, we'll see trees and grass and beautiful fields and running brooks. Better be ready!"

The driver was at the door. The animals crouched tensely. The doors swung open. When the animals peered out, their hearts sank. In front of them stretched a rainy city street lined with drab buildings. No trees, no green grass, no rolling meadows.

"The next stop," whispered Arletta encouragingly.

But the next stop was as disappointing as the last one.

Arletta crawled over to her friend.

"I've got an idea," she whispered. "There's no sense in both of us waiting here in hopes of seeing the country. A little flying squirrel like you can get along fine even in a big city." She leaned closer and spoke in a very confidential voice. "The next time that door opens, why don't you hop out and run for someone's back yard."

Ginger looked shocked. "Are you *crazy*? Are you telling me to leave you here alone?" She shook her head. "We are in this together, and together we'll get out of it."

The truck slowed down once again.

"Maybe this time," said Arletta hopefully. Ginger gave her an encouraging smile.

They could hear the driver getting ready to

open the door. The animals took up their positions. They didn't really expect too much. But when the driver swung open the doors, the animals got a wonderful surprise. Ahead of them and to their right lay a huge grassy field—with trees and bushes!

"Grass!" cried Arletta.

"Trees!" exclaimed Ginger.

The driver looked around, wondering at the strange noises coming from the back of the truck.

"Run!" cried out Arletta.

"Fly!" Ginger called joyfully.

Arletta swooped right between the driver's legs and tumbled off the truck. Ginger scrambled over the highest packages and swept past his nose. She spread her legs and soared out of the truck. Twenty feet through the air she sailed while the driver stared. "Oh, no!" he groaned, covering his face with both hands. "I didn't see it! I swear I didn't see it!"

Side by side they zoomed around a corner, skidding on the wet pavement. They scrambled over a low stone wall and plunged into a thicket. Panting hard, not even daring to believe they were safe, they looked at each other without a word.

And then the silence was broken. A voice

they had never heard before said, "Where did *you* come from?" Arletta and Ginger looked at each other in fright.

"Did you hear something?" inquired Arletta in a whisper.

"A voice. I heard a voice," said Ginger. "It asked where we came from."

Just then the voice called again. "What's the matter, cat got your tongue? Are you all right?"

Arletta spoke up. "Who are you? And what do you want?"

"My name is Orson. Stay where you are. I'm coming to join you."

And out from under a nearby bush stepped a skunk! Arletta thought he was very handsome. His coat was shiny black. A broad white stripe ran along the bridge of his nose and flared out into a magnificent wide streak down his back. His eyes were bright and alert.

Gracefully, the handsome skunk skipped through the rain and wriggled under the thick bush where Arletta and Ginger were huddled.

"I watched you running," he said. "You sure were in a hurry. I wondered whether you were in some kind of trouble."

Arletta answered: "I hope we are *out* of trouble. We just escaped from a delivery truck. And just before that we escaped from a department store."

Orson's eyes showed that he didn't quite believe it, so Arletta and Ginger had to tell him the whole story. When it was over, he gazed at them, fascinated.

"Well, well," he said. "You *have* had a time of it. But now your worries are over. I bid you welcome to the Bronx Zoo."

"A zoo!" exclaimed Arletta in a startled voice. "I didn't know that zoos looked like this!"

Orson smiled. "Well, actually you are not *in* the zoo, but very near it. All of this is the New York Zoological Park; I understand it is the largest one in the country. We are in the park area, and squirrels and chipmunks and other little animals roam free here. No one seems to mind the company of a skunk either, I am happy to say. At least I haven't been bothered, and I've been here quite awhile."

He turned to Arletta. "If I may say so, you are a most welcome sight. Until you arrived, I was the only skunk here. There's a cute little skunk named Petunia in the Children's Zoo, but

I am talking of full-grown country skunks like you and me."

"I thought the animals in the zoo were kept in cages," said Ginger. "Are they all free like you?"

"Oh, no, miss. There are *thousands* of animals here, and all different kinds. They couldn't all be allowed to go where they wished. But the zoo people provide good homes for them in cages and dens and houses, and they enjoy a very nice way of life."

He looked out at the rain. "You picked a miserable day to drop in. Not many humans come here on a day like this. But on sunny days they just swarm in to visit the animals and stroll through the park. And they feed those of us who roam around. Peanuts, popcorn, parts of sandwiches. Dropped ice-cream cones, cookies. All sorts of good things."

Ginger asked: "Is it fun living in the park? Is there a lot to do?"

"Oh, I keep busy. Watching the humans go by is very interesting. And it's always exciting to watch the zoo people bring new animals into the zoo. They brought a few in today. Let's see. There was a yak, a couple of reptiles, and one funny-looking fellow for the Small Mammal House."

"Could it have been an opossum?" asked Arletta hopefully.

"Why, of course! That's what it was! Long nose, gray hair sticking up all over him, skinny naked tail. Ugly chap."

"He is not!" said Arletta indignantly. "Anyway, would it be possible to visit him?"

"In the Small Mammal House? It's dangerous, but I suppose it could be arranged." He looked at Arletta curiously. "Whatever could a lovely skunk like you see in such a funny-looking animal?" he asked.

"He may be a friend of ours. We just *have* to find out." And so Arletta told Orson all about Norton's bravery in helping them escape.

"Well, in that case, I'll see what I can do. It may take time."

He looked out again at the rain. "But first I'd better do something about making you two more comfortable. Wait here, please. I'll be back for you."

Chapter 15

Orson spent a busy afternoon looking for a comfortable burrow for Arletta. He found a perfect place at the edge of a wooded area, under a rock that leaned solidly against a chestnut tree. Arletta was very pleased with it. The hole was deep and dry and well protected. There was a front entrance and an emergency exit. Ginger enjoyed scrambling up the tall trees and zooming down to sit on top of the rock. Both animals were already feeling at home in Bronx Park.

When Orson saw that they were comfortably settled, he went off to scout the Small Mammal House. He did a very thorough job, and by the time he had finished the rain had stopped and the gray afternoon was turning into evening.

He came back to the burrow and poked his nose into the hole. "Arletta," he called, "it's Orson. May I come in?"

"Come right in," answered Arletta. She had been busy widening the burrow into a nice-sized room and was tidying up the edges.

"I found a way into the Small Mammal House," said Orson triumphantly. "There's a drainpipe which leads from the floor of the house to the outside. It's big enough for us to crawl through. The drainpipe is covered inside by a metal grill, but one of the screws is missing from it. I can swing the grill out far enough so that Ginger can squeeze through it. With her pulling on the grill from above and my pushing it from underneath I'm sure we can turn it far enough for all of us to get through."

"Wonderful!" exclaimed Arletta. "Can we try it tonight?"

"Yes. We'll wait until it is good and dark, and then I'll lead you to it."

Arletta and Ginger were too nervous to relax. Ginger kept poking her nose through the hole to see how dark it was. Finally Orson said, "I think we can go now."

He led the way across the fields to the animal

house, avoiding the footpaths. Soon they came to the Small Mammal House. Orson went around to the side of the building and cleared the dirt away from the end of the underground drainpipe.

"I'll go in first, then Ginger, and then Arletta. Ginger will help me turn the grill."

One after the other the animals crawled into the drainpipe. When they came to the grill in the floor, Orson twisted it as far as he could. Then Ginger squeezed past him, slipped into the room, and tugged at the grill from above. With a rasping sound the grill swiveled on the screw and left a gap large enough for the skunks to get through.

When they were all inside the room, the animals looked around. The room was brightly lit. There was a flight of steps leading to a platform in front of the dens that lined the walls.

"Well, here goes," said Arletta as she climbed the steps. "Come on. Let's look." They walked along the narrow platform. Almost all of the other animals were asleep. As they passed each little glass cage Arletta peered in. If she couldn't see who was in it, she tapped on the glass until the animal came out to investigate. Many were animals Arletta and Ginger had never seen before. Orson pointed out the huge-eared, black-tailed jack rabbit and his neighbor, the kangaroo rat. They both came from the desert. He introduced Ginger to the Kaibab squirrel, telling her that the only place such squirrels were to be found was in the highlands of Arizona. Arletta and Ginger were fascinated and very much impressed by Orson's knowledge. As they walked along in front of the cages Orson showed them jumping mice from Australia and night monkeys from South America. "They're the only monkeys that sleep during the day," he informed them.

Arletta and Ginger were so interested in seeing the unusual animals they almost forgot what they had come for. So it came as a wonderful surprise when they found themselves in front of a den, looking into the face of their friend Norton.

"Norton! It's you! It's really you!" shrieked Arletta with joy.

"Arletta! And Ginger! I never thought I'd see you two again!"

"I'm so delighted to know that you are safe, Norton," said Arletta. "But I'm sad about your ending up in a zoo."

"I love it here, Arletta! The food is good

and I have nice neighbors. And for the first time in my life I really feel safe!"

The animals jabbered away happily for a long time, but finally Orson interrupted the conversation. "I think we'd better go now. We're disturbing the sleep of the other animals."

"All right, Orson," said Arletta. She turned back to the opossum. "Good-bye for tonight, Norton!" she called through the glass. Ginger happily flipped her tail at him.

"Now that you know the way in, come often!" requested Norton.

"We will! We will!"

Orson frowned. "Come ladies, please. We've been here long enough. We'll come back another night."

With a final wave to Norton, they went down into the drainpipe. Orson was careful to arrange the grill so that no one could tell it had been moved.

In a few minutes they were back outdoors. Ginger scurried ahead to look for an acorn. Arletta waited while Orson replaced the dirt over the pipe. As they walked along Arletta took a deep breath. The earth smelled fresh after the rain. She looked up at the dark sky. The moon had come from behind a cloud and spread a soft light over the fields of Bronx Park.

Arletta turned to Orson. "What a wonderful place to live," she said.

"Do you think you might like to stay here?" asked Orson.

"Yes, I would. I really would."

"I'm very glad to hear you say that," Orson answered softly as they walked across the wet grass to Arletta's new home.

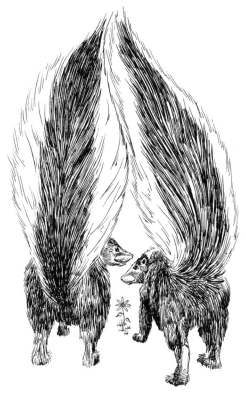

Format by Kohar Alexanian
Set in Linotype DeVinne
Composed by American Book–Stratford Press, Inc.
Printed by Halliday Lithograph Corp.
Bound by Haddon Bindery, Inc.
HARPER & ROW, PUBLISHERS, INCORPORATED